THE ROMAN MYSTERY SCROLLS

the
Two-Faced
God

Also by Caroline Lawrence

THE ROMAN MYSTERY SCROLLS

the Two-Faced God

CAROLINE LAWRENCE

Orion
Children's Books

First published in Great Britain in 2013
by Orion Children's Books
a division of the Orion Publishing Group Ltd
Orion House
5 Upper St Martin's Lane
London WC2H 9EA
An Hachette UK company

1 3 5 7 9 10 8 6 4 2

A catalogue record for this book is
available from the British Library.

ISBN 978 1 4440 0458 8

Printed in Great Britain by Clays Ltd, St Ives plc

www.orionbooks.co.uk

To my three grandsons:
Adrian, Jasper and August

CRASH!

The terrible noise jolted Threptus the soothsayer's apprentice out of a deep sleep.

From the henhouse next door came the muffled alarm-clucks of a dozen sacred chickens. 'Bk-bk-bk-bk-bk!'

Threptus leapt up from his low bed. As his

bare toes scrabbled their way into cold leather sandals, his mind raced.

Had the henhouse fallen down?

Had the temple behind them fallen down?

Had the whole seaport of Ostia fallen down?

He flung open the door of the one-roomed shack and peered out into the pre-dawn gloom of a winter morning. Apart from the sound of excited chickens, everything seemed normal. Flickering firelight showed the empty yard, the wooden chicken coop and the rear wall of the temple rising up solidly behind it.

Firelight?

As Threptus turned to find the source of the light, he saw a long dark head with tall pointy ears looming towards him over the fence.

'Aaaah!' cried Threptus, extending his left hand in the sign against evil.

'BK-BK-BK, B'KAK!' cried the sacred chickens from inside their coop.

'Hee-haw!' said the creature with the long dark head and tall pointy ears.

Threptus breathed a sigh of relief. It was only a donkey.

Holding a flaming torch, the donkey's owner

appeared from behind his cart. Imbrex the potter was the source of the flickering firelight.

'Great Juno's beard!' came a voice behind Threptus. 'What's going on out here?'

It was Floridius the Soothsayer. Like Threptus, he went to bed fully clothed apart from his shoes.

'Sorry!' said Imbrex. The torch showed his sheepish expression. 'Just wanted to drop the heads off as I promised. But I really did drop them. By accident,' he added.

Threptus spotted a big basket of lumpy objects lying just inside the fence.

'Ecce!' he said. 'There!'

'Euge!' said Floridius. 'Hurray!' He pushed past Threptus into the muddy yard.

Threptus followed and, in the flickering light of Imbrex's torch, he saw that the basket held a dozen human heads, their open eyes staring.

'Aaaah!' cried Threptus. Once again he extended his left hand, palm forward.

'BK-BK-BK, B'KAK!' echoed the sacred chickens from their henhouse.

'Hee-haw!'

'Don't worry, me little friend!' Floridius

patted Threptus's back. 'They're only painted clay busts.'

'Busts?' said Threptus. 'I thought that was something ladies had.'

Floridius laughed. 'A bust is a sculpture of a head, shoulders and part of a chest. See?' He reached into the basket and lifted out the bearded head and shoulders of an old man. Up close, Threptus could see it was made of clay, with black and white painted eyes staring spookily in the light of the torch.

Threptus reached out to touch the beaky nose and bulging clay eyes of the bust.

Then Floridius turned the head to show another face on the back, the face of a grinning child!

'Aaaah!' cried Threptus. 'It's got two faces!'

'BK-BK-BK, B'KAK!

Floridius nodded. 'That's right. This is Janus, the god of gates. He's got two faces so he can stand in a doorway and look outside and inside at the same time.'

'It's handy to see things from a different angle sometimes,' said Imbrex. 'Janus here is the only one of the gods who can see his own bottom.'

4

Threptus giggled.

Floridius said, 'Usually Janus is shown with his two faces exactly the same. But look! Ours are made especially for New Year's Day. The granddad's head shows the old year going out and the toddler is the new year coming in. Clever, isn't it?' he lisped.

Threptus nodded, even though the old-man face frightened him a little.

'I did 'em like you asked,' said Imbrex.

'Are they called busts because they're broken?' asked Threptus, lifting one of the two-faced heads from the basket.

'By Janus's bottom!' cried Floridius. 'It *is* broken. And so is that one!'

'Told you,' said Imbrex, backing away from the fence. 'I dropped the basket. But you should be able to glue them together with pine pitch.'

'We were going to ask ten sesterces each!' cried Floridius. 'I can't charge that for damaged goods.'

'Bk-bk-bk, b'kak!' scolded the chickens in their coop.

Imbrex shrugged. 'Caveat emptor,' he said. 'Let the buyer beware!' And with that he departed, taking his donkey, his cart and the flickering torchlight with him.

'Eheu! Alas!' came Floridius's voice in the darkness. 'I invested the last of me savings in this scheme.'

'Don't worry, master,' said Threptus, as he followed Floridius back into their dark shack. 'I'll help you glue them together.'

'You're a good apprentice,' came Floridius's voice.

Threptus groped his way to his bed. As he lay down, he almost squashed his kitten Felix, who had come to lie in the warm spot left by his body.

'Meow!' cried Felix.

'Sorry, Felix,' whispered Threptus, and moved the kitten over a little.

'Mrrrrow,' said Felix, who was very forgiving.

As Threptus stroked the kitten, he tried to think how he could help his master. Floridius was always lurching from one disaster to the next. His get-rich-quick schemes rarely worked. And whenever they did make some money, Floridius lost it by betting on chariot races.

'Master?' said Threptus into the darkness. 'Do you remember how you helped that little girl last month? And how her father said he would be your patron if you ever needed help?'

'Yes,' said Floridius. 'He was a banker named Liberalis.'

'Isn't a patron someone who helps you out?'

'That's right,' said Floridius. 'Patrons help their clients, and their clients do them favours in return.'

'Maybe you should ask Liberalis the banker if you could be his client.'

Floridius did not reply, but a few moments later Threptus heard him get up and start to move about.

'Where are you going?' asked Threptus.

'To take your advice,' lisped Floridius. 'Patrons usually receive their clients at dawn. Tomorrow is New Year's Day. What you do on the Kalends of January determines the course of the year. I'm not going to start this new year hungry and broke. I'm going to swallow me pride and ask Liberalis for a loan. I shouldn't be long. With any luck I'll be back in an hour with some warm honey cakes.'

'Euge! Yay!' whispered Threptus into Felix's ear. 'Warm honey cakes!'

But when two hours had passed and Floridius was still not back, Threptus began to worry.

SCROLL II

A LTHOUGH THE HOURS OF DAYLIGHT
were shorter in winter, they seemed very
long to Threptus as he waited for his master to
return. He had built up the fire in the portable
oven. He had said his prayers to the little wood
and clay household gods on their shelf. He had
let out the sacred chickens and fed them the
last few grains of barley. Sadly, it was mid-

winter and not one of them had laid an egg for breakfast.

Now Threptus was ignoring his growling tummy to do his homework. His assignment was to write a short report on the god Janus.

JANUS, wrote Threptus, IS THE GOD OF DOORS, GATES AND BEGINNINGS. HIS NAME IS LIKE THE WORD FOR DOOR. THE MONTH JANUARY IS NAMED AFTER HIM BECAUSE IT IS THE DOORWAY INTO THE NEW YEAR. JANUS'S SPECIAL POWER IS THAT HE HAS A FACE ON THE BACK OF HIS HEAD AS WELL AS THE FRONT, SO HE CAN SEE HIS OWN BOTTOM!

Threptus giggled. Then he remembered that Janus was the doorkeeper of heaven and sometimes he even made Jupiter wait to enter. Maybe he shouldn't joke about such a powerful god. Using the flat end of his stylus, Threptus rubbed out the bit about Janus being able to see his own bottom. Instead he wrote, BECAUSE SOMETIMES IT'S

HANDY TO SEE THINGS FROM A DIFFERENT ANGLE.

Threptus still had part of a wax tablet to fill, so he wrote this:

JANUS'S SPECIAL DAY IS THE KALENDS OF
JANUARY, THE FIRST DAY OF THE NEW
YEAR. ON THAT DAY WE GIVE PRESENTS TO
EACH OTHER, SUCH AS LAMPS OR HONEY.
FOR MY PRESENT I WOULD LIKE THE PAIR
OF FLEECE-LINED BOOTS I SAW IN THE
COBBLERS' MARKET.

Threptus sighed and rubbed out the last bit again. Floridius rarely had money and it would make him feel bad if he couldn't buy expensive fleece-lined boots. Instead, Threptus finished his report with a different kind of wish.

ON NEW YEAR'S DAY WE START AS WE
MEAN TO GO ON. I HOPE MY MASTER
FLORIDIUS WILL MAKE A GOOD START
AS A SOOTHSAYER, AND THAT I CAN BE A
DETECTIVE.

It was not a very long report, but Threptus was pleased. Two months ago he could hardly read, let alone write, and now he had filled one whole leaf of a wax tablet.

'Bweerp, bweerp?' Aphrodite the hen came through a low hole in the wall that Floridius called a 'chicken door'. She was making the soft croaking noise that told him she was exploring.

'Our master has gone to see a banker for help,' said Threptus. 'He's not back yet.'

'Brp, brp?' She had stopped to look at the basket.

'Those are clay busts of the two-faced god Janus,' explained Threptus. 'Master is going to sell them for the festival of the new year tomorrow.'

'Bk-bk-bk-bk!' It was Aphrodite's expression of mild alarm.

'Great Juno's beard!' exclaimed Threptus. 'You're right! People will want them for tomorrow! Floridius should be at his stall in the forum, selling them right now! Look after Felix and the other chickens,' he added.

The silky hen obediently hopped up onto the bed, fluffed her feathers and put her wing over Felix the kitten, even though he was almost as big as she was. Felix purred happily, his grey head just poking out from beneath her silky black feathers.

'Wish me luck!' cried Threptus, and he carefully stepped over the threshold with his right foot first.

He shut the reed gate of the yard behind him, so that no foxes or dogs could get at the chickens. Then he set off across the spongy waste ground towards the house of Liberalis.

There was a chill wind and his toes were already cold. Ahead of him some birds flew up from a flat-topped umbrella pine. Was it a good omen?

Tomorrow there would be the big new year's sacrifice of a heifer in the forum, the open-air centre of Ostia. Threptus's mouth watered at the thought of juicy pieces of grilled beef. As a beggar, he and his friends had always managed to get a few morsels from the share of the sacrifice set aside for the poor.

Now that he had someone to care for him, he might even get almond-stuffed-dates or a little pot of honey. His stomach growled at the thought.

As Threptus passed the south side of the forum he scanned it for any sign of Naso, the town bully, or his gang. He didn't see them, but he did notice that the forum was seething with happy shoppers.

Turning down Old Oak Street he spotted his master sitting beneath a columned porch outside one of the richest houses. For a moment the trunk of the holm oak outside hid him from view, but as Threptus got closer he saw that Floridius was resting his head in his hands.

'Master!' cried Threptus. 'The forum is packed! You should be selling your two-headed busts.'

Floridius lifted his head and shook it sadly.

'What's wrong, master?' cried Threptus. 'Are you still waiting for the banker to see you?'

'He's seen me.'

'Are you sad because he won't loan you money?'

14

'He loaned me the money.' Floridius reached into his coin purse, pulled out a bronze coin and gave it to Threptus. 'For your breakfast,' he said.

'Thank you, master.' Threptus's tummy growled as he put the coin in his battered leather belt pouch. 'So why are you sad?'

'His house is haunted. There have been strange goings-on here for the past few weeks. Food missing. Eerie bumps. Creaks from upstairs. Liberalis wants me to get an answer from the gods.'

'Euge! Hurray!' cried Threptus. 'Another haunted house mystery! We can keep a midnight vigil like we did for the perfume-maker's widow.' He shivered with a mixture of fear and delight at the thought of staying up late at night to catch a monster like the one that had haunted the sewer.

Floridius shook his head. 'He says he's already kept a vigil and found nothing. When I turned up this morning he said I was a godsend. He wants me to sacrifice a sheep.'

'Sacrifice? You mean *kill*?'

Floridius nodded. 'He wants me to examine its entrails for signs from the gods.'

'Entrails? You mean *guts*?'

Floridius swallowed hard. 'That's right. The horrible slimy, squiggly inside-bits of an animal. Brrrr.' Floridius shuddered. 'He's promised me one hundred sesterces and a new soothsayer's kit if I do it.'

'Euge! One hundred sesterces!' Threptus clapped his hands.

'Not Euge!' said Floridius. 'Eheu! It's a disaster. I haven't read the entrails of an animal since I was at soothsayer school.'

Threptus opened his eyes wide. 'But I thought soothsayer meant "gut-gazer".'

'There are two kinds of soothsayer,' said Floridius. 'A haruspex is a gut-gazer and an augur watches birds and nature. I'm an augur, not a haruspex. But when Liberalis told me that his brother has his very own private haruspex, I foolishly offered to be his!'

Threptus chewed his lower lip for a moment. Then he said, 'Why don't you go and sell your two-faced Janus busts now, and I'll try to find out what's haunting this house? If we solve the mystery, then you can tell Liberalis you saw the answer in the way the birds were flying or something like that. You will still earn your reward but you won't have to look at entrails!'

Floridius's grey eyes gleamed with hope. 'Yes! I could solve it as an augur, not as a haruspex!' Then he frowned. 'But he wants me to do the sacrifice tomorrow at dawn. Can you solve the mystery before then?

'Certe! Of course!' said Threptus. 'I love solving mysteries. Just like Lupus.'

Lupus was a mute ex-beggar boy who had solved many mysteries in Ostia before being sent into exile. He was Threptus's hero.

'Tell me about the mystery,' said Threptus. 'Are there any clues?'

'Yes,' said Floridius. 'Liberalis started hearing strange noises from the storeroom about a month ago, but whenever he looked in, it was deserted. And none of the other members of his household have heard a peep.'

'Maybe there's another creature in the sewers!'

cried Threptus. 'Like that one we found last month.'

'I doubt it,' said Floridius. 'The noises come from an upstairs storeroom, and sometimes it sounds like someone chanting.'

'Oh!' said Threptus. 'Maybe it's a larva: a ghost!' He left the shelter of the porch to go out into the street. From here he could see the windows on the upper floor. The window on the far right – by the tree – looked darker than the others. It was also barred.

'Is that dark window with the bars the storeroom?' asked Threptus.

Floridius nodded. 'That's it.'

Just then the double front doors of the house swung open and three people came out: a lady in an apricot-coloured palla, a plump slave-girl with a basket and a little girl in pink. The mother and her slave-girl looked neither right nor left as they set off along the pavement. But the little girl turned her head to look at Threptus and gave him a wide-eyed smile.

When the three had rounded the corner,

Threptus turned to his mentor and gave him a thumbs-up.

'Leave it to me, mentor,' he said. 'I'm going to solve the mystery!'

SCROLL III

THREPTUS HAD NEVER SEEN HIS OWN reflection, so he did not know that he was a good-looking boy. He had straight hair the colour of dark honey, long-lashed brown eyes and a ready smile. If he had not been dressed in a burlap tunic and second-hand sandals he might have passed for the son of a rich man. However, on this chilly winter morning, his olive green paenula covered his sackcloth tunic and he looked almost respectable as he caught up with the three females from the house of Liberalis.

'Salvete!' he greeted them breathlessly. 'Hello! I'm the soothsayer's apprentice. May I walk with you a little?'

'Is your master the one who cured our daughter by telling us to dedicate an altar to Fabulinus, the god of children's first words?' asked the mother.

Threptus nodded. 'Yes, domina,' he said politely.

'Then you are very welcome to come shopping with us. My name is Julia and this is my daughter, Marcella, who only spoke her first words last month. Say hello, Marcella.'

'Hello,' said Marcella. She had straight brown hair and hazel eyes. 'What's your name?'

'Threptus,' said Threptus.

'I'm almost four,' said Marcella. 'How old are you?'

'I'm not sure,' said Threptus, falling into step with them. 'But I think I'm almost nine.'

'We're having a feast tomorrow,' said Marcella. 'Will you come?'

'He'll be there anyway, dear,' said Marcella's mother. 'He's the soothsayer's apprentice.'

'Oh, look, Mama!' cried Marcella as they came into the forum. 'Honey cakes! I want a honey cake!'

Threptus saw Porcius, the plump son of Pistor the baker. Over the Saturnalia holiday, Porcius had started selling his father's pastries at a stall. Now he dispensed them from a tray on a strap around his shoulders. Today's selection included honey cakes and almond twists.

'Do you like honey cakes?' Threptus asked little Marcella.

'Yes!' She nodded enthusiastically.

'Me, too. But have you tried Pistor's almond twists? They look like thunderbolts!'

Marcella looked at Threptus wide-eyed. 'A thunderbolt looks like that?'

Threptus nodded wisely. He had recently learned all about thunderbolts, real ones as well as the ones made of pastry.

'Threptus?' said Marcella's mother. 'Would you like a pastry?'

'Yes, please, domina,' he said politely.

'Twist or honey cake?'

'Twist, please,' said Threptus.

Lady Julia fumbled for something under her palla and after a few moments she held out a big brass coin.

'Two honey cakes and two almond twists,' she said to Porcius, and put the sestertius on his wooden tray.

Porcius handed a honey cake to little Marcella, who took it eagerly.

Then he gave Threptus the biggest almond twist. 'From now on,' he said, 'I'm calling these "almond thunderbolts".'

Threptus generously broke off the tip and offered it to Marcella to try.

'Mmmm,' said Marcella.

Everybody laughed. Marcella's mother had the other almond thunderbolt and the slave-girl took the other honey cake. The four of them moved off a little and stood in a patch of mild winter sunshine, eating their pastries and watching the crowds in the forum.

'Ecce! Look!' cried little Marcella, excited crumbs flying out of her mouth. She pointed towards the north end of the forum, where a youth seemed to be walking on the shoulders of the people in the crowd.

'He's a stilt-walker,' said Threptus.

'What are stilts?' asked Marcella.

'Stilts are tall sticks you can stand on to make you taller,' Threptus told her.

The stilt-walker wore colourful clothes and a floppy orange Saturnalia cap. They watched until he disappeared behind the Temple of Jupiter, Juno and Minerva.

Marcella held her half-eaten honey cake out to Threptus. 'Trade?' she said, her mouth sticky with crumbs.

'Let Threptus eat his twist,' said Lady Julia. 'It's what he ordered.'

'I don't mind,' said Threptus. 'I love them both.' He cheerfully traded the remains of his almond thunderbolt for the rest of Marcella's honey cake. It was delicious, soaked in sweet honey and mixed with tangy cheese.

'Mmmm,' said Marcella, as she finished the almond twist. 'I like thunderbolts!' She slipped her sticky hand into Threptus's. 'And I like you,' she said.

Lady Julia laughed.

Threptus had an idea. 'Lady Julia,' he said. 'Would you like me to watch Marcella while you shop? We'll sit right here in the sunshine.'

'What a good idea!' cried Lady Julia. 'Rhoda and I need to get some eye ointment from the herbalist. Would you like to sit with Threptus, dear? You know how shopping tires you.'

Marcella nodded happily.

'Good.' Lady Julia bent down and used her handkerchief to clean the sticky crumbs from Marcella's chubby cheeks. 'Be sure to stay right there with Threptus, where I can keep an eye on you both.' Then she and her slave-girl set off towards the herbalist's stall by the Temple of Rome and Augustus.

Threptus and Marcella sat on a bench near the circular shrine at the centre of the forum. The bench was cold but the sun was almost warm. From here they could see everything. Threptus pointed towards the colonnade of the money-changers, where Floridius was showing a young couple one of the two-faced Janus busts.

Threptus pointed. 'See that chubby man at the end of the colonnade?' he said to Marcella. 'The one with the grey toga and lopsided garland? That's my master, Floridius.'

Marcella looked up at him wide-eyed. 'He's your master?'

Threptus nodded.

'Are you a slave?'

Threptus laughed. 'No, I'm an apprentice.'

'What's that?'

'It's like being at school. Only you live with your teacher. I'm learning how to be a soothsayer,' he added.

'What's that?'

'A soothsayer is a person who can tell what the gods are saying by looking at birds and clouds and lightning. And sometimes even entrails.'

'What's entrails?'

'Entrails means guts,' he said. 'The insides of an animal.'

'I saw a squashed squirrel one time,' said Marcella. 'It had entrails.'

'Yes,' said Threptus. 'Sometimes if an animal is squashed, the entrails will burst out.' The look on her face made him hurry quickly on. 'A soothsayer can also find out if a house is haunted. Last month, my master and I had to keep a midnight vigil at a widow's house because strange things were happening.'

'What's a vigil?'

'It's when you stay awake at night to look for strange things.' Threptus paused and said casually, 'Do strange things ever happen at *your* house? Like bumps in the night? Or food going missing? Or chanting?'

'No,' said Marcella. She pointed. 'Who's that man with the sticks and axe?'

'That's Bacillus the lictor. He walks in front of Bato, the magistrate. That bundle of sticks with the axe poking up shows that Bato is important.' Before she could ask what a magistrate or lictor was, Threptus said, 'Are you sure there are no strange noises in your house?'

Marcella nodded. 'I'm sure.'

Suddenly she stood up and pointed at a hunched old man in a yellow cloak on the far side of the forum. 'Proavus!' she cried. 'Great-grandfather!' Then she clapped her hand over her mouth and looked up at Threptus, her eyes round as coins.

But Threptus was not looking at Marcella or the old man in yellow.

He was looking up at the stilt-walker stumping towards them.

'Oi, you!' snarled the stilt-walker. 'I want a word with you!' And over his shoulder he called. 'Here he is, lads! I've found him!'

Threptus stared in alarm. The youth's pointy orange hat had disguised the fact that he had red hair.

It was his arch-enemy Naso, the town bully.

And Naso's gang was right behind him!

N ASO WAS COMING TOWARDS
Threptus and Marcella on his tall stilts. He
wore yellow leggings, a blue tunic, an orange
Saturnalia hat and a strange twisted expression
on his face.

Hurrying after him were his three young
henchmen: Quartus, Quintus and Mustela,
aged ten, eleven and twelve. Simple-minded

Quartus was neighing like a horse and causing startled citizens to recoil in alarm. Quintus was rolling a bronze hoop with little brass rings on it that jingled as they struck the stone paving slabs.

'Come on!' cried Threptus to Marcella. 'We have to hide!'

Grasping Marcella's sticky hand, he pulled her after him into the mass of shoppers. Marcella followed, giggling, as they wove this way and that.

Threptus could hear Naso calling, Quartus neighing and Quintus tinkling.

He looked around desperately.

Seven bald priests of Isis were proceeding towards the Marine Gate. They wore white sheaths and each one jangled a sacred metal rattle called a sistrum. Threptus and Marcella ran round the other side of them, then matched their steps to those of the priests, using them as a moving screen. Threptus jumped up to look between two of the priests and saw Naso, high on his stilts, moving in their direction. When the jingly priests reached the crossroads and kept going straight on the western road, Threptus grabbed Marcella's hand and pulled her along the road leading south.

When they reached the monumental stone entrance to a large covered market, Threptus tugged Marcella inside. This was Ostia's Macellum, where fish and meat were sold. Panting hard, Threptus and Marcella pressed their backs against one of the massive stone columns that flanked the entrance. Then Threptus heard the faint tinkling of a bronze hoop with sliding brass rings on it. He took a deep breath and peeked out into the street.

High on his stilts, Naso was stumping along, his head swinging right and left like a grim but colourful predator, in pursuit of his prey.

Only the week before, Naso had unexpectedly helped Threptus. But today he looked angry, and Threptus's ribs still ached from the last time Naso and his gang had kicked him. He did not want to risk another beating, especially with little Marcella under his protection.

He turned and glanced rapidly around, looking for the best hiding place. A high wooden roof made the meat market much dimmer than the open-air forum, even though there were lofty side windows. Threptus saw a long marble counter, a central fountain and side gutters to take away the blood. The fishmongers stood behind the marble counter, but the meat butchers had portable wooden tables in the central space around the fountain.

Immediately Threptus saw somewhere they could hide. One of the nearest meat stalls belonged to Brutus, and his youngest son, Lanius, was manning it. The stall consisted of a folding table covered in coarse burlap. Various cuts of meat were laid out on it, including a pig's head with half closed eyes.

Young Lanius had always been kind to Threptus. At the moment, he was talking to a lady in a tall wig. If Threptus and Marcella were quick, he would not even see them nipping underneath his table.

'Follow me,' he whispered to Marcella. He took her hand and they ran at a crouch to the table and darted underneath.

'Ugh!' muttered Threptus. He realised why Brutus covered the table with sacking: he had put all the inedible bits of meat and hoof down here.

'Ewww!' cried Marcella, pointing. 'Entrails!'

'You're right!' Threptus forced a bright smile. 'Those are entrails.'

'Why are we here?' she whimpered.

Threptus thought quickly. He didn't want to upset her. 'We're playing hide-and-seek with the boy on stilts and his friends,' he replied. 'Did you see them chasing us?'

Marcella put her thumb in her mouth and nodded.

'Let's see if we can spot them through the little holes in this cloth,' said Threptus. 'If we see any of them, we have to be very quiet. All right?'

Marcella nodded and the two of them brought their eyes close to the loose-woven burlap.

Threptus swallowed hard. He could see Naso towering by the fountain in the centre of the courtyard. He was turning on his stilts and glaring down at the stall keepers. Surrounding him were all three boys. Like Naso, they were also dressed in colourful clothes. Where had four beggar boys got hold of such expensive garments? Naso sometimes worked in the theatre. Had he stolen some costumes from a visiting troupe of pantomime dancers?

'See them?' whispered Threptus in Marcella's ear. 'That's why we have to be quiet. Just until they go.' He rubbed his left rib.

Marcella took her thumb out of her mouth. 'It smells under here,' she whimpered.

'Shhhh!' hissed Threptus. 'They'll hear you!'

'But it smells!' she repeated.

'I know,' he said. 'We'll go soon! Shhh!' Threptus's heart was banging hard, for he could hear the brassy tinkle of Quintus's hoop coming closer. He peeped through a hole in the burlap and saw Quintus, Quartus and weasel-faced Mustela coming his way.

'Oi,' said Mustela, coming right up to the table. 'You seen a little boy in a hooded green cape? We're looking for him. It's important.'

Threptus widened his eyes at Marcella and put his finger to his lips. She mirrored his expression with her own finger pressed to her sticky mouth.

'You mean Threptus the ex-beggar boy?' said the voice of Lanius the butcher's son from up above.

'Yeah,' said Mustela.

Threptus stopped breathing for a moment.

36

Lanius had seen him! Did the butcher's son know they were hiding under his table?

'I saw him run past the entrance just now,' said Lanius. 'He had a little girl in pink with him. They went that way.'

'Oi, Naso!' shouted Mustela. 'They went towards the Laurentum Gate!'

The three boys raced out of the Macellum and Naso stumped awkwardly after them, almost bumping his head on the arch.

Threptus breathed a sigh of relief and turned to grin at Marcella.

BANG!

BANG!

BANG!

Threptus and Marcella both jumped as something repeatedly struck the table only inches above their heads.

'There you are, domina,' said Lanius. 'Three nice boar chops for you.'

'Don't worry, Marcella,' said Threptus, his heart still pounding from the unexpected shock. 'It's only the butcher's son chopping up meat.'

But Marcella had started to cry. 'I want Mama!'

From the forum came the booming voice

of Praeco the town crier, made fainter by distance. 'ATTENTION, CITIZENS OF OSTIA. FOUR-YEAR-OLD MARCELLA, DAUGHTER OF MARCUS CLAUDIUS LIBERALIS, IS MISSING. SHE IS WEARING A PINK TUNIC AND PALLA! I REPEAT,' bellowed Praeco, 'A LITTLE GIRL IN PINK IS MISSING AND SHE MAY HAVE BEEN KIDNAPPED!'

SCROLL V

EVEN FROM HIS HIDING PLACE IN the covered market, Threptus could hear Praeco the town crier in the forum. His enormously loud voice was announcing the news of little Marcella's disappearance. 'A LITTLE GIRL' bellowed Praeco, 'BY THE NAME OF MARCELLA, IS MISSING. SHE MAY HAVE BEEN KIDNAPPED. HELP US

FIND HER. SHE IS DRESSED IN PINK. THE KIDNAPPER IS A BOY WEARING A GREEN, HOODED CLOAK.'

'No!' moaned Threptus. 'She hasn't been kidnapped! We were only hiding from the town bullies!'

Suddenly Threptus gasped as the burlap parted. A handsome upside-down face appeared. 'Praeco is calling you,' said Lanius the butcher's son. 'Also, it's safe to come out now. Those boys have gone!' His smiling face rose up out of sight.

Threptus pulled little Marcella out from under the table.

'Thank you,' he said to the butcher's son.

Lanius was looking at Marcella with wide green eyes. He opened his mouth to say something, but Threptus could hear Praeco calling so he pulled Marcella after him.

'MARCELLA! YOUR MAMA IS LOOKING FOR YOU! COME TO THE FORUM!'

Threptus and Marcella hurried back towards the forum.

As they ran down the stone-paved street

towards the main crossroads, three dogs that had been lurking near the entrance of the meat market began to trot after them.

'Why are those dogs following us?' panted Marcella.

Threptus glanced over his shoulder. 'You have a grey ribbon stuck to the bottom of your sandal. They're chasing that.'

Marcella started laughing. 'That's funny!' she said.

Threptus laughed, too.

By the time they reached the forum there were half a dozen dogs in pursuit.

'Here we are!' shouted Threptus, as they entered the forum. 'Marcella is safe with me. Look! Here she is!'

As they stopped running, two of the dogs started snapping at Marcella's heel. She stopped laughing and began to utter a high-pitched squeal.

A dozen citizens immediately rushed forward, but instead of thanking Threptus, one wrenched Marcella from his grip and another man grabbed him. 'Here's the culprit! Here's the boy who took her.'

'No!' gasped Threptus, held fast in the man's arms. 'We were only playing hide-and-seek!'

But Marcella's screams did not help his case. Two of the dogs were still fighting over the grey ribbon stuck to her sandal. Other growling dogs circled the crowd. Seagulls had begun to wheel overhead, adding their mocking cries to the commotion.

A man in a rust-coloured tunic kicked one of the stray dogs and pointed at Threptus. 'I know that boy,' he cried. 'Seen him begging in the Marina Market. He probably stole that fine cloak he's wearing.'

'No!' cried Threptus. 'My master bought it for me. I'm a soothsayer's apprentice now!' Held fast in a powerful grip, Threptus could barely breathe. He looked around for his master, but saw only angry faces.

Then the crowd parted to reveal Marcella's mother. Floridius was right behind her.

'My baby!' She cried. 'My baby!' And then she screamed. 'She's bleeding! What have you done to her?'

'Nothing!' cried Threptus. 'We were only

playing hide-and-seek! Mentor, tell Lady Julia I wouldn't hurt her little girl!'

But Floridius stood gaping like a fish. People around him were gasping, recoiling and making the sign against evil.

Threptus looked to see what had horrified them.

For the first time he noticed that the hem of Marcella's little pink tunic was soaked in blood from where she had crouched beneath the butcher's stall. There were also drips of red on her forehead where gore had seeped through cracks in the wooden planks of the table. But worst of all was the thing stuck to the sole of Marcella's sandal: the thing the two dogs were eating.

Threptus realised it was not a grey ribbon.

It was stretched-out entrails!

Marcella's mother staggered, her wrist to her forehead. But she managed to stay upright.

Of all the people crowding around, the only person to collapse in a faint was Floridius the Soothsayer.

SCROLL VI

T HERE WAS ONE GOOD THING ABOUT
Floridius fainting.

It made the man who was holding Threptus
loosen his grip for a moment.

Quick as Jupiter's lightning, Threptus twisted
out of his grasp. Then he charged through
the crowd and pelted down the Decumanus
Maximus towards the harbour. A few men

ran after him, shouting.

When Threptus reached the arch of the Marina Gate he raced straight through and out onto the beach. There was nowhere else to hide, so he plunged into the sea. He gasped at the coldness of the water.

Huddling down in the choppy little waves, with only his shivering head above water, Threptus looked back towards Ostia to see if anyone was still chasing him. From here he could see the white marble arch of the Marina Gate and the town wall with some red-tiled roofs peeping above. The stalls of the Marina Market were shuttered and silent. This part of Ostia was deserted because there was no sailing in winter.

Threptus waited as long as he could bear. When his teeth were chattering and his shoulders were shuddering, he came dripping out of the sea. A few strands of seaweed clung to his bare legs and wet sand gritted in his sandals. His olive-green hooded paenula was soaking. Once back up on the pebbly beach, he pulled off his sodden paenula, wrung out the seawater and put it on again. He was glad to see that the chilly salt water had rinsed away the blood from the butcher's stall.

Now his teeth were chattering and his toes were blue with cold.

The winter sun was shining but it did not have the strength to dry him. Threptus jogged across the sand dunes in an attempt to get warm. He ran past the tombs of the graveyard and at the dirt crossroads he took the fork leading to the Fountain Gate. Once inside the town walls he doubled back towards the Forum Baths. From his begging days he knew that the door to the furnace of the public baths was usually open. If the fire-slaves were nice, they would let you linger there to get dry.

But when he rounded the corner at the back of the baths, he saw someone sitting in the best place between the woodpile and the open furnace door.

It was the old man in yellow. He was a hunchback.

Threptus had never been this close to a hunchback before and he couldn't help staring.

The man wore a dirty yellow cloak, grimy tunic and mismatched sandals on his feet. He was very old, with a long grey beard and a hooked nose. He looked a little like the old-man face of the Janus bust.

Threptus swallowed hard.

Maybe the old man *was* the god Janus. Maybe he had come to Ostia in disguise to test the kindness of the citizens on the last day of the old year!

Floridius had told Threptus that the Greek gods Zeus and Hermes had once visited the earth disguised as ordinary men. They had gone looking for food and shelter. Everyone had cruelly turned them away. Only a poor old couple named Baucis and Philemon were kind enough to welcome the disguised gods into their home.

When Zeus returned to his home on Mount Olympus, he sent a flood to destroy all the people who had been mean to him. All except Baucis and Philemon, whom he spared.

'Come closer.' The hunchback was beckoning Threptus with a claw-like hand. 'Seems like you need the heat more than me. I'm just cold. You look cold *and* wet.'

Cautiously, Threptus went to stand near the hunchback near the hot opening of the hypocaust, the giant furnace beneath the warm rooms of the baths.

The intense heat made Threptus's woollen paenula start to steam. He sneezed.

'Salve! Good health!' said the hunchback, giving the proper response.

'Thank you,' said Threptus. 'Where's the fire-slave?' he added.

'Gone to pee, I think,' said the old man. 'I'm Gibber, by the way. Want to rub my hump?'

Threptus stared.

'Don't be shy,' said Gibber. 'It will bring you good luck. Only a quadrans,' he added.

Threptus did not want to offend a god in disguise and he needed good luck. He fished in his greasy, leather belt pouch and pulled out the shiny coin Floridius had given him. It was a coin called an 'as' and it was so new that it showed the Emperor Domitian who had only been in power three months. The as was worth four times what Gibber was asking, but Threptus knew it would be an insult to ask for change.

'Here you are,' he said, and placed the coin in Gibber's outstretched palm.

A toothless smile lit up Gibber's wrinkled face. 'Oh, thank you!' he said, and added, 'Stroke away. I don't mind. It's the only time people ever touch me.'

Threptus leaned over and stretched out his hand. For a moment he hesitated. Then he took a deep breath and stroked Gibber's back. Beneath the grubby yellow cloak, the hump felt bumpier than it looked, and sent a shiver through him.

'Oh, that's nice,' said Gibber. 'Feels nice to be stroked. Especially by someone with such a gentle touch.'

Threptus's paenula was already steaming and he knew it would soon be warm and dry. He turned back and forth in front of the furnace in order to warm himself all over, and used alternate hands to stroke Gibber. The hunchback had his eyes closed and a smile on his face. Was he a god in disguise? Or a real hunchback? Suddenly Threptus remember something Marcella had said.

'Are you related to Marcus Claudius Liberalis the banker?' he asked the hunchback.

Gibber opened his eyes and frowned. 'Never heard of him. Why do you ask?'

'I was sitting with his daughter in the forum earlier. She saw you and pointed and I think she called you proavus, "great-grandfather".'

Gibber pursed his toothless mouth, frowned and shook his head. 'I grew up in Rome. Only arrived here in Ostia last month. Never spoken to any bankers apart from the ones who give me coins for a lucky rub.'

'Oh,' said Threptus. 'Well, you were on the other side of the forum when she said it. She must have mistaken you for someone else. Or maybe I didn't hear right. She's only four.'

'Oi, you!' said a man in a scorched loin-cloth.

It was the fire-slave, back from peeing, and Threptus could tell straightaway that he wasn't one of the nice ones.

'Get away from there!' yelled the fire-slave, and – seizing a small log from the wood pile – he charged towards Threptus.

ONCE AGAIN, THREPTUS WAS PELTING
through the streets of Ostia in order to
escape a pursuer. But he knew the fire-slave was
not allowed to stray from his post and soon he
slowed from a run to a jog. When he reached
his shack he found his master was still out, so he
sat on the ramp leading up to the chicken coop
to catch his breath and plan his next move. The

sacred hens moved around his feet, giving their contented whiny purr.

When he felt Aphrodite's silky feathers brush against his bare ankle, Threptus picked her up and put her on his lap. He was already hungry for lunch, and still a little damp, but stroking her made him feel better.

She sat patiently on his lap and began to purr.

'I'll bet that poor hunchback would like a nice hen to stroke,' he murmured.

'Wrrrrr, brrrk,' she said very softly.

He bent his head. 'My plan went wrong,' he whispered. 'I was supposed to ask Marcella about some missing food and strange noises in her house. But she kept asking *me* questions!'

'Wrr, wrrk, brrrr,' croaked Aphrodite sympathetically.

'Then Naso and his gang came to bully me,' said Threptus, 'and when I took Marcella somewhere safe, everyone thought I'd kidnapped her. And then she got blood all over her tunic so maybe her parents won't allow Floridius to do the job tomorrow! But how can he do it anyway? He must be the only haruspex in the world who faints at the sight of blood and guts.'

'Wrrrr?' asked Aphrodite.

'A haruspex,' explained Threptus, 'is a kind of soothsayer who looks at the guts of dead animals to see what the gods are saying.'

'Bk-bk-bk-bk!'

'Don't worry,' said Threptus hastily. 'We'd never look at *your* entrails. You're too precious to us.'

'Wrrrooooow,' purred Aphrodite.

'I need to help my master,' said Threptus. 'I have to find out what's making the strange noises in Marcella's house, or I have to figure out a way for Floridius to learn how to examine the entrails of a sheep without fainting. Or both. Here he comes now. And he doesn't look happy.'

Floridius appeared with a heavy basket and a downcast face. Threptus put down Aphrodite and ran to open the gate.

'I only sold two Janus busts all morning,' said Floridius. 'And I had to bring me price down to sell those.'

'I'm sorry I made you faint,' said Threptus, closing the gate after him. 'Marcella and I were hiding from some bullies. Was her mother

55

very upset? Did she tell you not to come tomorrow?'

Floridius shook his head. 'I wish she *had* told me not to come. But Marcella explained that you were just playing hide-and-seek, so they're still expecting me to perform the sacrifice at dawn.'

Threptus opened the door of their shack and Floridius put the heavy basket of Janus busts on the floor near the oven. 'What possessed me to claim I could be a haruspex? If I can't even look at a few entrails in the market, how will I be able to study a sheep's liver?'

'Or cut its throat,' added Threptus.

'A haruspex doesn't do the sacrifice himself,' said Floridius. 'He usually gets his slaves to do that, or hires an assistant: somebody who is good with animals. But who?'

'Brk-brk, brrrrrrrk,' said Aphrodite, wandering into the shack.

Threptus looked at her. 'Aphrodite, that's brilliant! It might just work!'

'What?' said Floridius.

'Why don't you ask Lanius the butcher's son to be your assistant?' said Threptus. 'He can do

56

the sacrifice and all you have to do is read the liver.'

'I don't know,' said Floridius. 'He's very young.'

'He's grown a lot in the past few months,' said Threptus. 'He has muscles now.'

Floridius heaved a sigh. 'Worth a try, I suppose. Where can we find him?'

'He was at a stall in the meat market about an hour ago. If we hurry we can catch him before it closes.'

*

'How did Aphrodite make you think of Lanius?' asked Floridius as they hurried through the forum a little later.

Threptus said, 'She said "Brrrk", which sounds a bit like "Brutus". That made me think of Brutus's son, Lanius. He's nice. He helped save me from the bullies earlier.'

It was almost noon and, when they reached the Macellum, most of the stall-holders were beginning to pack away, but Lanius was bargaining with a man for his last piece of meat.

When Floridius saw the pig's head, he averted his eyes.

The pig's head didn't bother Threptus. He was used to such sights.

'You can look now, master,' whispered Threptus as Lanius wrapped the pig's head in a piece of burlap.

'Hello, again,' said Lanius to Threptus. He lowered his voice. 'Did you escape disaster?'

Threptus nodded. 'Thank you for sending those boys away.'

'I was happy to help,' said Lanius. 'That Naso has too much time on his hands. He should get a job.'

'This is my master,' said Threptus. 'Aulus Probus Floridius, soothsayer. He has to sacrifice a sheep tomorrow.'

'Do you have any?' asked Floridius.

'Yes, sir,' said Lanius. 'My father can sell you a sheep without blemish for twenty sesterces. Bath and ribbon included.'

'That's a fair price,' said Floridius. 'Also . . . I am officiating at the sacrifice tomorrow, but I need an assistant – someone who can perform the actual sacrifice. Will you do it for twelve sesterces?'

The youth's green eyes lit up. 'I would be honoured to perform the sacrifice for you!' he said.

Floridius handed over eight silver denarii. 'Can you bring the sheep to the house of Marcus Claudius Liberalis, the banker, at dawn tomorrow?'

'Liberalis lives on Old Oak Street, right?'

'That's right,' said Floridius. 'His house has a porch with two columns and a double door.'

'It's right by the old holm oak tree,' said Threptus.

'I'll be there!' said Lanius. 'Father keeps saying I'm too young, but I've been practising and I know I can do it.'

'How old are you?' asked Floridius.

'Fifteen,' said Lanius. 'Well, almost fifteen. I can also help you read the entrails,' he said quickly. 'I've been teaching myself how to read livers for the past few months.'

'You have?' said Floridius. He and Threptus exchanged excited looks.

'Yes,' said Lanius. 'I even have a clay model of a liver with Etruscan writing on it. But don't tell father. He thinks only a high-born person can become a haruspex. He told me not to get my hopes up.'

'You have the Etruscan liver model?' cried Floridius. 'The bronze one?'

'No,' laughed Lanius. 'Mine is crude and made of clay, but it has all the signs on it.'

'May I see?'

Lanius glanced around, fished down the front of his tunic and pulled out an object the size of his hand. It looked like the leather sole of a shoe – flattish and oval – but unlike a shoe it had three bumps on it, and also some writing and lines that must have been scratched into the clay when it was still wet.

'I study it when I'm not working,' explained Lanius.

Threptus had been learning to read and write for over three months but when he bent over the model of the liver he could not read one word.

'What does it say?' he asked.

'It's Etruscan,' said Floridius to Threptus. 'Nobody knows.'

'I think I do,' said Lanius. 'Do you see how the lines divide up the non-bumpy half of the liver into six sections, the way you slice a pie?

60

That's a map of the heavens! If you see a spot on the liver you have to identify what section it's in. If it's in this section nearest the middle of the liver, then it has to do with health.' He pointed to the other sections in order. 'Or it could be love, family, piety, money or travel. Do you see? If the mark is milky, it means it's to do with someone close to you. If it's dark then it has to do with you, or whoever sponsored the sacrifice. There's more, but those are the basics. Did you follow?'

Threptus nodded excitedly. But Floridius looked confused.

'Wait,' said Lanius. 'I'll show you. I'm supposed to deliver a liver after the market closes. He reached under the table and pulled out a plate. 'Here it is: a real sheep's liver. Now can you see these little marks here on the shiny surface . . .'

THUD!

Floridius had fainted.

SCROLL VIII

ON THE WAY HOME, FLORIDIUS began muttering to himself. 'Don't know what's wrong with me,' he said. 'First I faint at a bit of blood and then the sight of a liver knocks me out. What's wrong with me? Oh, why did I say yes to Liberalis?'

To Threptus's dismay, Floridius began to cry: big fat tears rolling down his unshaven cheeks.

Threptus had never seen Floridius weep before.

He had never seen any adult cry.

Threptus felt his own eyes prick with tears.

'Don't cry, master,' he said. 'Just tell him you can't do it.'

'But I've already spent half the money he gave me to buy the sheep,' said Floridius.

'Lanius is nice. He'll give it back.'

'I've spent some of the money on other things, too,' confessed Floridius.

Threptus's spirits sank. His master's weakness was spiced wine and betting on the horse races. They would never get *that* money back.

'If I don't fulfil my part of the deal,' said Floridius, 'then Liberalis could take me to court and have me sent to the mines.'

Back at their one-roomed shack, Threptus made Floridius lie down. He unlaced his master's sandals and covered him with his cloak. He added wood to the portable oven. Finally, he moistened a handkerchief with water from the rainwater barrel outside and pressed it to his master's swollen eyes.

'Wait here with Felix and the chickens,'

he said, going to the door. 'And don't worry!'

'Where are you going?' said Floridius in a feeble voice.

'I'm going to be a detective,' said Threptus. 'A sneaky detective like Lupus. I'm going to find out what's haunting Liberalis's house so you can earn your fee without having to sacrifice that sheep tomorrow!'

Before his master could object, Threptus was hurrying towards the house of Liberalis.

He needed to see inside that storeroom. Were the bars wide enough for him to squeeze through? If he couldn't get inside, could he at least peek in? He would have to climb the old holm oak near Liberalis's townhouse.

Old Oak Street was quiet. Everyone was eating lunch or at the baths. Threptus ran to the big oak tree, quickly glanced around and then swarmed up it like a monkey. Safe in the shelter of the leaves, he found a branch that stretched towards the storeroom window.

Going as far as he could, Threptus parted some of the smaller branches. He could see the window but nothing inside.

His heart sank. It was no good. He would have to think of another way.

As he started to move back, he heard an angry chittering from the leaves above him. He tipped back his head and saw a squirrel on a higher-up branch.

Could a squirrel be the culprit?

A squirrel could easily leap from the branch to the window and pass through the bars into the storeroom. Little Marcella had seen a squashed squirrel, so there might be more than one living in this tree.

A family of squirrel thieves would explain most of the noises Liberalis had heard, and the missing food.

Threptus looked up at the squirrel. 'I'll bet you're the thief, aren't you? All we have to do is put shutters on that storeroom window.'

The squirrel chattered angrily at him.

Then came another noise. A noise that made Threptus's heart skip a beat. It was the merry tinkling of brass rings on a bronze trundling hoop. Then came an even more frightening noise: the *thump, thump, thump* of wooden stilts on paving stones. The thumps were getting louder and louder, closer and closer.

Threptus closed his eyes and held his breath and prayed to Janus that Naso and his gang wouldn't find him.

For a moment the thumping stopped.

Then came the most terrifying sound of all, a loud rustling such as a giant squirrel might make.

Threptus turned his head.

'Ahhhh!' he yelled, and nearly tumbled out of the tree.

The head of red-haired, red-faced Naso loomed only inches from his.

'Got you!' said Naso, pushing aside an annoying branch. 'What you doing up here? You trying to break into one of these houses?'

'No,' stammered Threptus. 'I was just trying to see in that window.'

'Spying on ladies?' Naso smirked.

'No!' cried Threptus. 'The house is haunted and I'm trying to find out what it could be.'

Naso batted aside a twig that was poking him in the eye. 'Well, get down. The boys and me want a word with you.'

Threptus's arms and legs were trembling as he climbed back down out of the tree. As he hung from the lowest branch, about two feet from the street, he formed a plan. He would hit the road running, speed away from Naso and then dart down the alley by the wall fountain. Naso couldn't follow him there on his stilts.

Threptus let go of the branch, landed lightly and turned to run.

The three boys blocked his way. Quintus brandished the brass trundling hoop and stick like weapons.

Threptus glanced around to see if there were any kind citizens around. But the street was deserted.

'Don't even think about running,' said weasel-faced Mustela.

'Yeah,' said Quintus, trying to look mean. 'Don't even think.'

And simple-minded Quartus added, 'Bk, bk, bk, bk!'

Threptus stiffened. He was not a chicken; he was not afraid. Even though he was only eight years old and they were all older and bigger, he could put up a fight.

He made his hands into brave fists and stood with his own feet planted shoulder's width apart and his jaw set.

'Calm down, me old son!' Naso jumped down onto the street. His stilts leaned against the lowest branch of the oak. 'We ain't going to beat you. I only want to talk. I been looking for you all day.'

'Why?' Threptus was still glancing around for means of escape.

'Fact is, me old son,' said Naso, 'that you've inspired us. Me and the boys want to turn over a new leaf. Want to stop begging and stealing and get ourselves a paying profession.'

Threptus stared. 'Do you want to be detectives, too?'

'Detectives?' Naso frowned. 'Don't even know what that means. No, me old son, we want to be acrobats.'

'Acrobats?' said Threptus.

'Yeah,' said Naso. 'I can do stilts and tightrope on account of I got no fear of heights, and me boys can tumble through a hoop. Show him, lads.'

Threptus stared in amazement as Quintus

used the stick to make the tinkling hoop run around him in a circle while Mustela tumbled through it. Then the two older boys faced each other, bent at the waist and, with the hoop around them, they made their backs into a kind of table. Simple-minded Quartus clambered on top, said, 'Cock-a-doodle-doo!' and did a backflip dismount. He stumbled awkwardly and ended up sitting on his bottom. 'B'kak?' he said.

The boys laughed – even Quartus – and Threptus couldn't help giggling, too.

'We want to start tomorrow, on New Year's Day,' said Naso, 'but that snooty magistrate, Bato, warned us he would take us to court as we don't have a licence. I asked him how to get a licence. He said, and I quote, "If you can get a single person to write you a recommendation I will grant you a temporary licence." So you see,' said Naso, 'I need a recommendation.'

'From me?' said Threptus.

'No, not you, blockhead! Your master, Floridius, the chubby chicken man.'

'Can't you ask someone else?' said Threptus.

'No, I cannot ask somebody else,' said Naso.

'For some reason they have all taken against us in this town.'

'Why don't you go to Rome?' suggested Threptus.

'You trying to get rid of us?' said Naso.

'A little bit.'

'Ha, ha, ha. Now will you get your master to write me a note or not?'

Threptus looked at the stilts leaning against the oak tree. Then he looked at the storeroom window of Liberalis's house. He was almost positive the culprit was a squirrel, but for Floridius's sake he wanted to be sure.

He turned back to Naso.

'I will ask my master to write you a letter,' he said, 'if you go to that window and tell me if you see squirrel droppings on the windowsill or floor.'

'You want me to get up on me stilts and go see if squirrels have been pooing in that house?'

'Yes, please.'

Naso scowled at him. 'What if the owners come back? If they take me to court I'll never get permission to be an acrobat.'

Threptus looked at the stilts. 'If you're afraid, then let me have a go.'

'I ain't afraid. Quintus! Mustela! Come here and bend over.'

The two older boys went to the stilts and bent at the waist again. Naso used their backs as a platform to mount the stilts. Once aboard, he clomped out from under the shelter of the tree and over to the storeroom window.

Threptus and the boys followed.

'Squirrel poo is rounder than rat droppings,' Threptus whispered up to Naso.

'I don't see no— Ahhhhh!'

The boys on the street saw the terrible face at the window at the same moment as Naso. It was an old man's face like that of the Janus head, with a hooked nose and a white beard, glaring at them with terrible milky-blue eyes.

'Ahhhh!' cried the boys, and made the sign against evil.

Naso staggered back on his stilts, thrown off balance by his terror. He tottered for a moment, and Threptus had to jump sideways to avoid being knocked down.

Threptus fell, but Naso managed to stay aloft

and was soon clomping rapidly down the street, fleeing at a forward-leaning angle with his three boys leading the way.

Threptus scrambled to his feet. His heart was pounding with fear, too, but for the sake of his master he wanted to know what was up there.

He took a deep breath, made the sign against evil and looked back up at the window.

It was empty. As if nothing had ever been there.

Could it really have been the god Janus? Was it a demon? Or a larva? Had they surprised an ancient burglar? Could it have been Gibber the hunchback? Threptus shook his head. Gibber's eyes were keen and dark. He had only glimpsed the face in the window for a moment, but he remembered the eyes had been milky-blue, almost as if they couldn't see.

One thing was certain. The culprit was definitely not a squirrel.

SCROLL IX

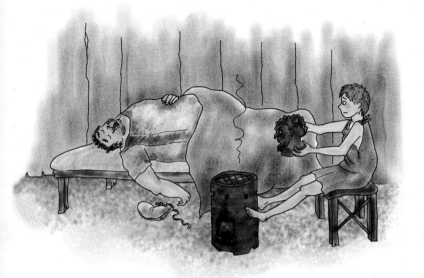

WHEN THREPTUS GOT BACK TO HIS shack he found his master fast asleep and snoring. There was an empty wine-skin beside the bed.

It was just as Threptus had feared: Floridius had been spending money on spiced wine.

That was bad. When Floridius got sad, he

75

drank wine. Wine made him sleep and then he didn't earn money and that made him even sadder, so he went out and spent their precious money on wine again. It was like a hoop going round and round. A bad hoop of despair.

Threptus put the last few pieces of wood in the clay oven and took off his sandals and put his freezing bare feet right up against the warm clay. His toes were so cold he could barely feel them. He must go and scrounge an old pair of socks from one of the rubbish tips outside the town walls, but old socks were almost impossible to find at this time of year.

He stared sadly down at the basket of cracked Janus busts on the floor beside him. Without taking his feet from the outer wall of the oven, he took one of the two-faced heads out and rested it in his lap. It was cracked but still in one piece.

Janus was lucky. He could see before and behind, the future and the past. He could look at things coming and going. Threptus sighed. If only he could look at things from a different point of view, maybe he would find an answer to their problem. Threptus turned the bust to look at the child's face.

For some reason, the child's face reminded him of his hero, Lupus, the young beggar turned detective who had gone away a few months before.

What would Lupus do?

Immediately Threptus knew: Lupus would make a list of clues and try to solve the mystery that way.

Threptus replaced the bust and pulled his wax tablet out of his belt pouch. With the young face of Janus looking up at him from its basket, he wrote,

WHAT IS THE THING IN THE STOREROOM OF LIBERALIS?

   I. FOOD MISSING – PROBABLY NOT A GHOST AS THEY DON'T EAT.

   II. CHANTING – PROBABLY NOT A SQUIRREL AS THEY DON'T CHANT.

   III. OLD MAN'S FACE IN WINDOW – BURGLAR? BEGGAR? GOD IN HUMAN FORM?

IV. OLD MAN LOOKED BLIND. LADY
JULIA BOUGHT EYE OINTMENT.
SHE KNOWS ABOUT HIM?

V. MARCELLA CALLED HUNCHBACK
'PROAVUS'. HUNCHBACK LOOKS
LIKE HER GREAT-GRANDFATHER?

VI. HUNCHBACK LOOKS LIKE OLD
MAN IN WINDOW – OLD MAN
IN WINDOW MARCELLA'S GREAT-
GRANDFATHER?

VII. LADY JULIA KNOWS ABOUT OLD
MAN BUT LIBERALIS DOESN'T.

VIII. ANSWER TO THE MYSTERY: LADY
JULIA IS HIDING HER GRANDFATHER
FROM HER HUSBAND!

Threptus looked at his wax tablet in amazement. He hadn't known the answer until he'd started to list the clues. But now he did!

'Thank you, Janus,' he whispered to the bust. He closed his eyes. 'And thank you, too, Lupus. Writing things down helped me solve the mystery!'

Or had it?

Was his answer the right one?

He had to find out if his theory was correct.

For the third time that day, Threptus set out for the house of Marcus Claudius Liberalis on Old Oak Street. He took the cracked but whole Janus bust from the basket. It had been good luck for him so far. It could be his lucky talisman, like the sword of Theseus or the bow of Ulysses.

Outside, the sky had clouded over and a breeze brought the smell of rain.

As Threptus turned onto the street, he saw a rain shower coming his way.

Quickly he wrapped the Janus bust in a fold of his cloak. 'If I can reach Liberalis's house without getting wet,' he told himself, 'it will be a good omen.'

A few drops spattered the pavement just as he ran under cover of Liberalis's columned porch.

Had any of the drops touched him? He thought not.

He knocked on the door.

The door opened and a skinny slave stood looking down at him. He held a wooden spoon in one hand and wore a sauce-stained apron. From this Threptus guessed he was a cook.

'Good afternoon,' said Threptus politely, 'I

have brought a new year's gift from Floridius the Soothsayer. Is your master in?'

The slave merely shook his head and started to close the door.

'Threptus!' said Marcella, running into the atrium. 'Let him in, Cocus!' she cried.

'But your parents are out and your mother told me not to—'

'He's my friend!' Little Marcella stamped her foot. 'Let him in!'

Cocus shrugged and went back to the kitchen.

Carefully stepping over the threshold with his right foot first, Threptus entered a lofty atrium. It had red and yellow painted panels on the plaster walls, marble columns and cedarwood benches. Its centrepiece was a rectangular pool of water beneath an open skylight: an impluvium and a compluvium.

Threptus moved forward wide-eyed.

It was raining inside! As the sun came out from behind a cloud, the drops falling through the open skylight to the rectangular pool below made a rainbow.

'Look!' said Threptus to Marcella. 'A rainbow

in your house. It must be a good omen!'

'What's an omen?' asked Marcella.

'An omen,' replied Threptus, 'is a sign from the gods.' Before she could begin asking questions he unwrapped the Janus head from a fold of his cloak. 'Look! I brought you a present for the new year.'

'Great-grandfather!' said Marcella. 'Proavus!' Once again, she clapped both hands over her mouth as if she had said something wicked.

'Marcella,' said Threptus. 'Does this Janus head look like your great-grandfather?'

Marcella just looked at him, her hazel eyes wide above the hands still covering her mouth.

'Marcella,' he said gently, 'is your great-grandfather secretly living in your upstairs storeroom?'

Marcella continued to gaze at him with coin-shaped eyes.

'Don't be afraid,' whispered Threptus. 'Look!' he tipped his head towards the rainbow above the impluvium. 'It's a good omen. The gods aren't angry. They're happy.'

Marcella's gaze slid sideways to look at the

rainbow. Then she looked back at him.

'You don't have to speak a word,' said Threptus. 'Just nod or shake your head. Is your proavus living upstairs?'

Marcella took her hands away from her mouth and nodded.

'Will you take me to him?'

Without speaking a word, Marcella clutched his right hand and pulled him after her. Cradling the Janus head in his left arm, Threptus obediently followed the little girl. They went out of the atrium, along an unpainted corridor, through a small kitchen and up dark and narrow stairs.

At the top, Marcella pushed open a wooden door and they stepped inside.

Lit only by the small, barred window, the storeroom was dim and stuffy. It smelt of salt pork, rosemary, thyme and urine. Threptus could see amphoras leaning up against one wall and a cedarwood chest against another. There were some wooden crates, a ladder, pots of paint and a broken chair. Hanging from the ceiling were some haunches of meat and bundles of herbs.

'Proavus!' whispered Marcella. 'Proavus, I've brought you something.'

A wooden lid of one of the crates opened and the face of Janus rose up from inside it.

'Aaaaah!' cried Threptus.

Even though he had been expecting to see the scary face from the window he was not prepared for this.

Marcella's great-grandfather was the oldest person he had ever seen. He was even older than Gibber the hunchback. He was bald, with wrinkled skin, a big nose and a beard just like Janus. His eyes glared but did not see: both pupils were covered with a milky-blue film. He clambered awkwardly out of the crate, groping with his hands and staring with unseeing eyes.

Little Marcella went to him and hugged his knobbly knees. He stroked her soft brown hair with a gnarled hand.

'Who's here?' croaked the ancient man. 'Who've you brought?'

'It's my friend Threptus,' said Marcella. 'He helps the soothsayer.'

'You weren't supposed to tell anybody about me!' said the old man in his cracked voice. 'You're supposed to leave me up here to die!'

'Don't be cross,' said Marcella. 'Threptus brought you a present.'

Threptus stepped forward and held out the clay head so that it just touched the tips of the man's fingers. The old man began to feel it, then seized Threptus's wrist and pulled him close. Threptus tried not to tremble as the old man's fluttering fingertips tapped his face like doughy moths.

'Just a little boy,' quavered the old man. And to Marcella, 'Your Threptus is just a boy.'

'Why are you hiding up here, sir?' asked Threptus in a shaky voice.

'My granddaughter's husband doesn't like me,' said the old man. 'And she is ashamed of me. Since my wife died, nobody knows what to do with me.'

Now his big hands were exploring the clay head of Janus. As he felt the side with the child's face, he smiled. Then he found the old man's face on the back. His own toothless mouth gaped open.

'What is it?' he quavered.

'It's a clay bust of the two-faced god Janus,' said Threptus. 'The old man is the old year and the child the new one.'

'No!' moaned the old man.

CRASH! The bust had slipped from his tremulous grasp. It broke in two.

'It's a bad omen,' cried the old man. 'It's a sign I'm going to die tomorrow, on New Year's Day!'

And tears began to dribble from his sightless old eyes, down his wrinkled cheeks and into his beard.

SCROLL X

'MASTER! I'VE SOLVED THE MYSTERY of the haunted house!'

Half a dozen chickens scattered as Threptus flung open the door of the one-roomed shack.

Floridius was sitting on his bed, examining the contents of a cedarwood box. 'You have?' he said. 'You've solved the mystery?'

'Yes! The thing making bumps and chanting

and eating food is Marcella's great-grandfather. Marcella's mother smuggled him in a month ago and she's been waiting for the right moment to tell her husband.'

'Why would she hide her grandfather?' Floridius's speech was slurred.

Threptus scooped water from the rainwater barrel by the outside of the door and gave the cup to his master. 'I'm not sure. Maybe because he's wrinkled and blind and scary-looking and Marcella says he pees himself sometimes. I think Lady Julia is afraid Liberalis will be angry that she took him in.'

Floridius drank the water and shook his head sadly. 'Rich people,' he lisped. 'I will never understand their ways.'

Threptus said, 'I think we should tell Liberalis the gods want him to be nice to his wife's grandfather.

'Bweerp!' agreed Aphrodite.

Threptus picked up Aphrodite and stroked her. 'We can use the sacred chickens!' he said. 'Or clouds! Or an inside rainbow.'

'Too late,' said Floridius miserably. 'We have to do the sacrifice.'

Threptus frowned. 'But the whole point of me finding out what was haunting the banker's house was so you could solve the mystery as an augur, not a haruspex!'

'Bk, bk, bk!' agreed Aphrodite.

'I know,' said Floridius, 'but it's too late. Look what Liberalis just sent me.' He held up a fine woollen tunic the colour of sea-foam: palest green. It was Threptus-sized.

Threptus put down Aphrodite and stepped forward to touch it. 'Is that for me?' he breathed.

Floridius nodded. 'He sent ones for me and Lanius, too. And I got a fine new toga worth at least fifty sesterces! And look,' he pointed to the shelf where they kept their own household gods. 'Freshly woven garlands.'

'Oh!' breathed Threptus. He went to the shelf and reached for the smallest of three garlands. It was green and glossy, and its sweet scent made him happy.

Floridius pointed to the small cedarwood chest. 'And this is the most expensive gift of all.'

Threptus went to the cedarwood box on his master's lap and looked inside. It contained six bronze items: a jug, a little bucket, a flattish bowl, a box, a tray and a sharp, triangular knife. 'They're beautiful,' breathed Threptus. 'What are they?'

'They are the tools of the haruspex. Fine priestly implements, worth about two or even three hundred sesterces.'

'It's like you're a real haruspex!' breathed Threptus.

'I know,' quavered Floridius. 'To send these wonderful things back would be a horrible insult to Liberalis. Lanius can use these to sacrifice the sheep, but I'm the one who has to read the omens.'

'But how, master?'

'I don't know!' wailed Floridius.

'Master,' said Threptus, 'haven't you ever been to a sacrifice?'

'Lots of times. But it's getting worse as I'm getting older. Now I stand at the back and close me eyes. Oh, I wish I were blind.'

'Master! Don't say such a thing!' Threptus made the sign against evil and spat three times for extra good luck.

On the bed, Felix the kitten was exploring Floridius's fine new toga. Even folded up, the piece of cream-coloured woollen cloth was vast. Threptus could see the bump made by the kitten as he moved haltingly underneath.

Abruptly, his little head poked out. Threptus giggled at the sight of the kitten with his head covered by a toga.

That was when he got the idea.

'Eureka!' he cried. 'I think I know how you can be a gut-gazing haruspex without fainting tomorrow!'

THE FIRST DAY OF THE NEW year dawned chilly and bright. A glaze of frost on the red roof tiles made Ostia look sparkly pink to the birds flying overhead. Wood smoke rose from a thousand hearths. The sound of flutes and tambourines filled the air, along with cheerful cries of 'Happy New Year!'

Parents gave their children fig-leaf parcels of a dozen dates. Patrons gave their clients candles or oil lamps. Masters gave their slaves a few coins to spend on pastries or trinkets.

And Threptus had found new fleece-lined boots at the end of his bed!

'That's why I couldn't back out of being a haruspex,' Floridius told him. 'I bought those boots as soon as Liberalis gave me the money.'

'Master, they're wonderful.' Threptus felt his eyes brim with tears. 'How did you know?'

'I saw you eyeing them in the Cobblers' Market last week,' said Floridius.

Threptus eagerly put on the boots. They were only a little too big and the fleecy lining made them cosy and warm.

'I also got a pair of woollen socks in case they're too big.' Floridius held out a pair of pale orange socks.

'Now they're perfect,' said Threptus. 'With my nice woollen paenula I'll always be warm.' He fished under his mattress. 'I only got you this belt pouch,' he said. 'I found it on the rubbish tip outside the Laurentum Gate, but I cleaned it and mended the hole myself. See? I made the thread say F for Floridius.'

'Just what I needed!' said Floridius. He had been to the baths the evening before and for once his cheeks were smooth. He wore his new sea-foam-green tunic and the fresh garland over his fluffy clean hair.

'Now we'd better hurry,' he said. 'Will you help me put on me toga?'

Threptus had never seen a toga spread out before. It looked like a huge oval blanket made of cream-coloured cloth. He could barely hold it all, but Floridius told him which bit to put over his arm and which bit to put under.

At last Floridius was ready.

'How do I look?' he asked.

'Like a real soothsayer!' said Threptus. 'And me?' He wore a pale green tunic, soft leather boots with a creamy fleece lining and the dark green garland on his tawny hair.

'Like a real soothsayer's apprentice,' said Floridius.

By the time they reached Liberalis's house they could see the household assembling and a brazier full of coals flaming below the oak tree. Lanius wore only a wreath, a loincloth and sandals. His tanned, oiled torso looked strange on this frosty morning. He was leading a clean sheep with a red ribbon tied around its middle.

Threptus and his master stood near a tripod of glowing coals and warmed their hands. The fragrant scent of saffron rose up, woody and sharp. Threptus was not wearing his paenula so his arms had gooseflesh. But his new boots meant his feet were warm.

'Are we all here?' asked Floridius.

'Not quite,' said Threptus, rubbing his arms. 'The musicians are on their way.'

'Musicians?' said Floridius.

'Yes,' said Threptus, at the sound of a flute and silvery tinkling. 'So that no unlucky noise be heard before the sacrifice. Listen, I think I hear them now!'

Around the corner came Naso and his gang. They were wearing their colourful tunics and making a joyful noise. Quartus was playing a four-note tune on Threptus's homemade pan-pipes. Quintus was rolling his tinkling hoop. Weasel-faced Mustela was jingling a sistrum and Naso was banging a tambourine.

They stopped playing when they reached the holm oak and Naso came right up to Threptus.

'Hello, me old son,' he whispered in Threptus's ear. 'We ain't late, is we?'

'You're just in time,' said Threptus. 'Stand by Lanius. You're assisting him.'

'Righty-ho!'

Quartus started to play his breathy pan-pipes.

'Not now!' hissed Quintus. 'Wait until they start to walk!'

Quartus nodded, wide-eyed. For once he made no animal noise.

'If everyone is here,' said Floridius, 'then let us begin.' He put a fold of his toga over his garlanded head. 'Hear me, O Janus! And thou, O Jupiter!' he cried. 'We, the family and friends of Marcus Claudius Liberalis, gather before you to celebrate this first day of the new year and to bless it. As the sheep is sacrificed we ask you to reveal the truth of what is haunting this house.'

He turned to Liberalis.

'The gods have told me that you must proceed to the crossroads and sacrifice the sheep there. If this house is possessed, I will see the demon fly out as the life-blood flows. The two children will help me,' he added. 'Their eyes are clear.'

'Are you sure?' said Liberalis. 'That's not the usual practice.'

Floridius closed his eyes and raised his hands. 'Humm. Umm. Bummm,' he said, intoning his magic words. He opened his eyes. 'Yes, I am sure. If it is not a demon haunting your house, I will be able to tell you when you return with the liver.' He took the toga from his head and stared intently at the window.

'Very well,' said Liberalis.

The procession set off towards the crossroads. Liberalis led the way, followed by Lady Julia and her slave-girl, Nutrix. Lanius and the sheep went next, followed by Cocus the cook. Naso and his gang took up the rear, playing a solemn but jingly tune.

When the small procession was out of sight, Floridius turned to little Marcella, who had stayed behind with the two of them. 'Watch the window carefully,' he said to her, and he winked at Threptus.

Marcella stared at him wide-eyed, then gazed back at the storeroom window.

From the branches of the oak came the chittering of a squirrel.

'Squirrel!' cried Marcella and then giggled.

Half an hour later, the procession returned, all except for Lanius.

'Your assistant did a wonderful job,' said Liberalis, who was holding the liver on a plate. 'He's still by the crossroads, butchering the sheep. Was there a demon?'

'No,' said Floridius, keeping his eyes on the window. 'The strange noises must be caused by something else. Give the liver to Threptus. He will bring it to me.'

Liberalis handed the plate to Threptus. On it lay the brownish-red sheep's liver. It was smooth, slippery and steaming a little.

Threptus's knees were shaking as he took the plate to Floridius. He knew if he dropped the liver it would be a terrible omen. The sacrifice would have to be done all over again!

Once again, Floridius covered his shaggy head with a fold of his toga. To everyone else it looked as if his head was bent over to study the liver. But Threptus was standing right below him. He could see that his master's eyes were shut tight.

This was the idea Felix the kitten had given Threptus: that the squeamish soothsayer cover his head and keep it lowered so that nobody could see his eyes were closed.

'Hmmm. Ummm. Bummm.' Floridius chanted in his favourite magic language and waved his hands dramatically. 'O Janus, we praise you,' he cried with his head still down. 'For the auspices are good! The liver shows wealth and happiness for the year to come.'

Everyone murmured happily and gave a polite smattering of applause.

'But wait!' proclaimed Floridius dramatically, keeping his head still down but raising up his right arm. 'There is a blemish in part of the liver to do with family life. The gods say that you, O Liberalis, are not caring for someone in your household.'

Liberalis frowned. 'I don't understand,' he said. 'What can that mean?'

'I am not sure. Let me look.' Only Threptus could see his master's face squinched and his eyes tightly shut. 'Hmmm. Ummm. Bummm,' intoned Floridius. 'I see a respected ancestor. And woeful neglect.'

'Alas!' cried Liberalis. 'Whom have I neglected? Which ancestor have I wronged?'

At this his wife knelt on the cold paving stones of the street. 'O husband, it is I who have done wrong!' she cried. 'It is my guilt! My aged grandfather came to Ostia last month and begged me to take him in. But you always said you disliked him. So I have been hiding him upstairs, waiting for the right moment to ask you. Will you forgive me and let him live with us?'

'What?' cried Liberalis.

'Let Proavus out, Tata!' cried little Marcella. 'Please let him out!'

'By Hercules! How long has he been there?'

'Almost a month,' said Lady Julia, who was now in tears.

'What can I do?' Liberalis asked Floridius.

'How can I make this right?'

'Hmmm. Ummm. Bummm,' said Floridius, waving his hands. 'You must accept him into your family. Give him a fine room and make his last days comfortable.'

Floridius's head was down and his eyes still closed. But he was gaining confidence and waving his arms about dramatically. This was a mistake. For as he waved his hands, he knocked the plate from underneath so that the liver flew up into the air!

Threptus and all the others watched open-mouthed as the liver went up, up, up and then began to fall down, down, down . . .

Jang! Naso caught it inside his tambourine!

For a moment there was silence.

'It's a good sign!' cried Threptus. 'It shows you can save things at the last moment.'

'Yes!' cried Liberalis eagerly. 'Disaster averted.'

Everyone cheered and patted Naso on the back and said 'Well done!' His freckled face was red with pleasure.

Cocus stepped forward. 'I'll take that,' he said. 'It will make nice kebabs.'

Naso gave him the tambourine and Cocus took it into the house.

'We did it, master!' whispered Threptus to Floridius, and added, 'You can open your eyes now.'

SCROLL XII

THREE HOURS LATER, AS THE GONGS clanged noon on the first day of the year, the sound of feasting, laughter and music could be heard in the atrium of Liberalis's townhouse. The double doors were wide open on this day, special to the god of doors and new beginnings. The sun shone through the skylight of the atrium and made the colourful tiles on the bottom of the impluvium sparkle.

Most of the banker's clients were here, plus some of his neighbours.

With a napkin tucked into the neck of his fine new tunic, Threptus sat on a bench beside his mentor and ate morsels of tender lamb roasted on skewers, washed down with spiced honey-water. It was delicious.

Old Proavus was the guest of honour. He had no teeth for chewing but he had drunk three bowls of mutton broth. For desert he ate honey by the spoonful from a little white jar. When his son-in-law asked him to live with them and promised to take him to a doctor who could restore his sight, he danced a jig of joy.

The duumvir Bato was also here, with his mother, the Lady in Lavender, and his young fiancée. Lucilia looked pretty in a pale yellow tunic with a fringed peach-coloured palla. She had her little lap dog on a silken lead.

Fourteen-year-old Lanius was speaking with Bato. The butcher's son had used a street fountain to wash the blood from his head, arms and torso. His black hair was slicked back and he wore the third new sea-foam-green tunic that Liberalis had sent to Floridius. The colour brought out the green in his long-lashed eyes.

Even Naso and his gang were here. They had given Floridius's letter of recommendation to Bato and Lucilia was clapping her hands and laughing at their antics. Naso was stilt-walking around the atrium while the other three tumbled through the jingly hoop or did somersaults. After Quartus ended up in the impluvium for the third time, Lady Julia invited the acrobats to stop and eat. The boys eagerly ran to the table and devoured the remaining food. And when Liberalis gave each of them a sestertius as payment they cheered.

But the happiest guest of all was the hunchback Gibber. Threptus had spotted him drinking from the wall fountain near the old holm oak and invited him back for the feast. Nobody minded because Threptus told them it was good luck to stroke a hunchback, and *double* good luck on the first day of the year.

Everyone had stroked Gibber's hump and now he sat happily on a stool, knee to knee with old Proavus. They had both grown up in Rome and were talking about the good old days. Proavus was holding little Marcella on his lap. She had been hugging him but now she was looking over his shoulder at Lanius, who was playing with Lucilia's lap dog.

'The butcher's son will make a good haruspex,' said Floridius through a mouthful of raisins.

'Lanius?' said Threptus.

'Yes. I am going to give him me box of implements.'

Threptus stared. 'You're going to give those bronze things to Lanius? But you said the box was worth two or three hundred sesterces!'

'We've done a deal,' said Floridius. 'In return, Lanius has promised to give us a choice cut of meat three times a week for the next two years. The good thing about that is that I can't gamble it away.'

Threptus clapped his hands and Floridius added. 'Gods willing, we'll never go hungry again.'

They both spat and made the sign against evil.

'Also,' continued Floridius, I've told Liberalis that Lanius would make a much better haruspex than me. I'm going to stick to birds, clouds and lightning.'

'And sacred chickens,' said Threptus. 'Live ones, not dead!'

Floridius laughed and ruffled his hair. 'That's right, me little friend,' he said. 'Sacred chickens, alive and clucking.' He heaved his bulk up from the bench. 'I'm off to get a refill,' he said. 'Honey-water, not wine. I mean to start the new year right.'

As his master went to refill his cup, Threptus watched little Marcella. She was leaning over her great-grandfather's shoulder. With her young face beside the old man's they looked like Floridius's version of the two-faced god Janus!

This reminded Threptus of all his answered prayers.

He closed his eyes. 'O Janus,' he whispered, 'thank you for making everything end happily. Please will you help me solve more mysteries this year, so that I can carry on Lupus's good work?'

He opened his eyes just in time to see blind old Proavus and four-year-old Marcella turn their heads towards him. They were both smiling and it seemed as if the two-faced god Janus had said 'Yes'.

*

A few days later, on the Nones of Januarius, Threptus was writing Lupus an account of how he'd solved the mystery, when a mud-spattered messenger knocked on the door of their one-roomed shack.

'I've got a letter for Threptus the apprentice of Probus Floridius,' he said, 'who resides in a shack abutting the Temple of Rome and Augustus. It's from the great port of Ephesus in Asia Minor,' he added.

Threptus jumped up in excitement. He knew only one person in Ephesus: his hero.

He did not recognise the seal with a tiny lady reading a scroll, but as soon as he saw the writing on the piece of papyrus, he knew he was right.

It was a letter from Lupus!

He opened it with trembling fingers and read . . .

From the former owner of a wax tablet, to Threptus in the port of Ostia:

Greetings! I got your letters. They both arrived together. Because the sailing season will not begin for three months, I am sending this letter by land. Here is an important message for you. I hope you understand it: 'Will Baucis and Philemon receive visitors for the Floralia?' I hope the answer will be 'Yes'. I leave you with this request. 'Longingly search the horizon as Aegeus once did, but for green not white.' Vale. P.S. Keep the seal on this letter. It is important.

Floridius was peering over his shoulder. 'What does it mean?' he asked.

Threptus looked up at his mentor, wide-eyed. 'I'm not sure. But I think it's code. And if I'm right, it means Lupus is coming back to Ostia!'

Find out how the adventures began in . . .

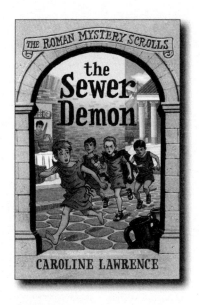

Threptus, once a beggar boy in the
Ancient Roman port of Ostia, has joined
forces with Floridius – freelance soothsayer,
and dealer in sacred chickens. Now he finds
himself struggling to outwit the law, solve
mysteries and even fight 'demons'!

The adventure continues in . . .

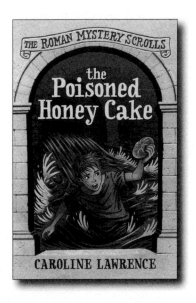

Floridius, freelance soothsayer,
is afraid that he has lost his talent for
seeing the future. Threptus wants to
find some titbits of information that his
mentor can use to convince people he still
has the gift, but will a poisoned honey
cake lead to disaster along the way?

THE ROMAN MYSTERY SCROLLS

Don't miss . . .

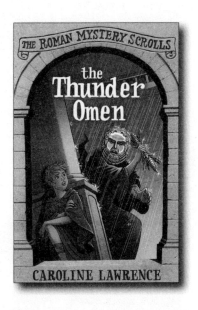

It is Saturnalia – the topsy-turvy midwinter
festival of feasting and fun – but Floridius seems
beset by bad luck. One of his prophesies failed
and now he has a powerful enemy!

Amid the plays, pantomimes and
pandemonium, can Threptus find a way
to give everyone something to celebrate?